First American Edition 2018
Kane Miller, A Division of EDC Publishing

Text copyright © 2017 Alice Rex
Based on an original idea by Angela Perrini
Illustrations copyright © 2017 Angela Perrini
First published in Australia 2017 by New Frontier Publishing Pty Ltd
Translations rights arranged through Australian Licensing Corporation

Library of Congress Control Number: 2017942229
Printed and bound in China
2 3 4 5 6 7 8 9 10
ISBN: 978-1-61067-712-7

Kane Miller
A DIVISION OF EDC PUBLISHING

For Luke, forever a light in my heart. AR

For Dad, Mum and Valeria, with all my love. AP

AVA'S
spectacular
SPECTACLES

Alice Rex & Angela Perrini

Ava sat at her desk, gazing at the board.

"Ava," said Mrs. Cook. "Where are your glasses today?"
Ava looked down at her schoolbag.
She hated her glasses.

Mrs. Cook picked up a large book
and opened it in front of Ava.

"If only Little Red Riding Hood had put on her glasses the day she went to visit her grandmother!" said Mrs. Cook.

"She would have seen the big teeth and big eyes."
Ava looked up. Mrs. Cook turned the pages.

"Imagine if Hansel and Gretel had worn their glasses when they got lost in the woods. They would have seen the signs pointing them safely home."

Ava looked brighter.

"Everybody knows Humpty Dumpty's sad story, but if he had put on his specs, he would never have fallen off that wall."

Ava nodded and added, "If the king's horses and king's men had worn their glasses, they would have been able to put him back together again!"

"And have you heard of little Bo-Peep who
lost her sheep?

"She never lost them at all! With glasses, she would have seen those woolly faces all around her.

"And if little Miss Muffet had been wearing her glasses,

she would have seen that big spider and used her bug spray!"

Ava reached into her schoolbag and
pulled out her glasses.

The letters written on the board became clear, and the words made sense. Ava could understand whole sentences!

She smiled and began to read.